W9-CHV-777

1864
CHANGES FOR
Addy
A Winter Story

By CONNIE PORTER

ILLUSTRATIONS DAHL TAYLOR

VIGNETTES RENÉE GRAEF, GERI STRIGENZ BOURGET

★ American Girl®

THE AMERICAN GIRLS

1764  KAYA, an adventurous Nez Perce girl whose deep love for horses and respect for nature nourish her spirit

1774  FELICITY, a spunky, spritely colonial girl, full of energy and independence

1824  JOSEFINA, a Hispanic girl whose heart and hopes are as big as the New Mexico sky

1853 CÉCILE AND MARIE-GRACE, two girls whose friendship helps them—and New Orleans— survive terrible times

1854  KIRSTEN, a pioneer girl of strength and spirit who settles on the frontier

1864  ADDY, a courageous girl determined to be free in the midst of the Civil War

1904  SAMANTHA, a bright Victorian beauty, an orphan raised by her wealthy grandmother

1914  REBECCA, a lively girl with dramatic flair growing up in New York City

1934  KIT, a clever, resourceful girl facing the Great Depression with spirit and determination

1944  MOLLY, who schemes and dreams on the home front during World War Two

1974  JULIE, a fun-loving girl from San Francisco who faces big changes—and creates a few of her own

Published by American Girl Publishing
Copyright © 1994, 1998, 2000 by American Girl

Questions or comments? Call 1-800-845-0005, visit **americangirl.com**,
or write to Customer Service, American Girl, 8400 Fairway Place, Middleton, WI 53562.

Printed in China
12 13 14 15 16 LEO 26 25 24 23 22

PICTURE CREDITS
The following individuals and organizations have generously given permission to reprint
illustrations contained in "Looking Back": p. 53—Schomburg Center for Research in Black Culture,
The New York Public Library, Astor, Lenox, and Tilden Foundations; pp. 54–55—Library of
Congress (Richmond and voting images); Howard University, Moorland-Spingarn Research Center;
pp. 56–57—Farm Security Administration, U.S. Department of Agriculture; Urban Archives,
Temple University, Philadelphia, PA; Photographs and Prints Division, Schomburg Center for
Research in Black Culture, The New York Public Library, Astor, Lenox and Tilden Foundations;
pp. 58–59—National Portrait Gallery, Washington, DC/Art Resource; Magnum Photos Archive,
New York, NY; National Museum of American History, Smithsonian Institution, Photo by
Louis P. Plummer (pennant); Collection of David J. & Janice L. Frent (button); pp. 60–61—UPI/
Bettmann (children entering school and Selma march); Fred Ward, Black Star (March on
Washington); National Museum of American History, Smithsonian Institution,
Photo by Louis P. Plummer (button).

Cover Background by Dahl Taylor

Library of Congress Cataloging-in-Publication Data

Porter, Connie Rose, 1959–
Changes for Addy : a winter story / by Connie Porter ; illustrations, Dahl Taylor;
vignettes, Renée Graef, Geri Strigenz Bourget.
p. cm. — (The American girls collection)
Summary: With the end of the Civil War in 1865, Addy desperately hopes that her family will
be reunited in freedom in Philadelphia, but the future may hold both happiness and heartache.
ISBN 1-56247-086-8 (hardcover). — ISBN 1-56247-085-X (pbk.)
1. Afro-Americans—Juvenile fiction. [1. Afro-Americans—Fiction. 2. Slavery—Fiction.
3. Family life—Fiction. 4. United States—History—Civil War, 1861-1865—Fiction.]
I. Taylor, Dahl, ill. II. Title. III. Series.
PZ7.P825Ch   1998   [Fic] — dc21   98-16817   CIP   AC

TO MY EDITOR,
BOBBIE JOHNSON—
THANKS FOR HELPING
BRING ADDY TO LIFE.

TABLE OF CONTENTS

ADDY'S FAMILY
AND FRIENDS

POPPA
*Addy's father, whose
dream gives the family
strength*

MOMMA
*Addy's mother, whose
love helps the family
survive*

ADDY
*A courageous girl,
smart and strong,
growing up during
the Civil War*

SAM
*Addy's sixteen-year-old
brother, determined to
be free*

ESTHER
*Addy's two-year-old
sister*

AUNTIE LULA
The cook on the plantation, who has always looked out for Addy's family

UNCLE SOLOMON
Auntie Lula's husband, who gives good advice

SARAH MOORE
Addy's good friend

MRS. MOORE
Sarah's mother, who helps support her family by taking in laundry

MRS. FORD
The firm-but-fair owner of the dress shop where Momma works

PIECES OF A PUZZLE

On a wet and windy afternoon in early December, the door to Mrs. Ford's shop flew open. Addy and Sarah rushed inside. The door slammed shut behind them so hard it rattled the windows.

"We sorry, Mrs. Ford," Addy and Sarah said together.

"Well, don't just stand there dripping on the floor, girls," Mrs. Ford said briskly. "Go over to the stove and dry off."

Addy's mother smiled from where she sat at the sewing machine. "Y'all late getting here from school," she said. "It's so cold, I thought you'd run all the way."

"We stopped by the Quaker meeting house to see if Mr. Cooper had any news about Esther, Auntie Lula, and Uncle Solomon," said Addy. "But he didn't."

Momma took off Addy's hat and smoothed her hair. "Well, we just got to hope he hear something tomorrow, then," she said.

"He probably won't," said Addy with a sigh. She peeled off her mittens and held up her hands to the warmth of the stove. More than a year ago, Poppa and Sam had been sold off Master Stevens's plantation and Addy and Momma had run away, leaving baby Esther behind with Auntie Lula and Uncle Solomon. The war had been over since April, and Poppa and Sam had joined them in Philadelphia. But Addy's dream of having her *whole* family together in freedom was taking a long time to come true.

Poppa had gone back to the Stevenses' plantation last summer to find Esther, Lula, and Solomon, but they had left, and no one knew where they'd gone. Poppa had searched several freedmen's camps near the plantation, but after a month, he had returned to Philadelphia. Since then, Addy had helped write letters each week to aid societies and freedmen's

2

camps to see if anyone, anywhere, knew anything about her family. But no one ever answered.

"I know you feeling discouraged," said Momma kindly. "But we can't stop hoping. The only way you get what you want is by hoping and working hard."

"Your mother is right," Mrs. Ford said. "And she has been working hard. We both have. With the new sewing machine, we'll make twice as many dresses as we did by hand."

"And that mean me and Addy gonna have twice as many dresses to deliver!" said Sarah.

"And that means we gonna make twice as much tip money," said Addy with a smile.

The whole Walker family was saving money so Poppa could make another trip to search for Esther, Lula, and Solomon.

"There's plenty for you girls to do today," said Mrs. Ford. "In addition to the deliveries, I need you to pick up two dresses for alterations and go to the dry goods store."

"We better get started then," said Addy, putting on her mittens and hat.

But Sarah wasn't ready. She was taking off her boots. "Mrs. Ford, I don't mean to bother you, but

do you got any extra paper for me to put in my boots?" she asked.

"Child, what you need is another pair of boots," Mrs. Ford said.

"Sure do, ma'am," Sarah said, pulling wads of dirty, wet paper out of her boots. "These is too small, but my folks can't afford to buy me new ones yet. I'm gonna get new soles for these. That's cheaper."

Addy saw that Sarah's stockings were wet to the ankle. There was a hole as big as a half dollar in one boot, and the sole was nearly ripped off the other. Mrs. Ford handed Sarah the newspaper.

Sarah took a few minutes to fold it and stuff as much of it as she could into each boot, and then she pulled her boots back on.

"The paper should last till I get home," Sarah said, "if I don't slop through too many puddles!"

The girls gathered the packages Mrs. Ford had wrapped and headed for the door.

"Y'all take care crossing the streets," Momma reminded them.

"We will," they promised.

"And for goodness' sake, don't let the door slam!" Mrs. Ford added.

Addy smiled at Mrs. Ford and made sure she closed the door quietly as she and Sarah left the shop.

It wasn't sleeting now, but there was still a strong wind. The streets were crowded with people rushing along, trying to get out of the cold. Addy held her armful of packages close to her chest to keep them safe.

"The first address is over on Commerce Street," she said to Sarah. Addy turned right as they came to the corner, but Sarah turned left.

"Where you going?" Addy asked, catching

hold of Sarah's sleeve. "Commerce Street is this way, past Washington Square."

"You right," Sarah said, smiling. "I don't know what I'm thinking." As she and Addy walked along together, Sarah went on, "Things sure done changed since last year. Back then, you would turn the wrong way, not me. You hardly knew anything about Philadelphia back then."

Addy smiled. "You the one who taught me how to find my way around," she said. "I couldn't even read the addresses on the packages."

"Now you read better than me!" Sarah said. "That's why Reverend Drake gave you the most important part to read in the celebration at church on New Year's Eve."

Addy made a face. "I'm kinda nervous about that," she admitted. "The Emancipation Proclamation is hard! It's got big words in it I don't even understand."

"I can help you practice," said Sarah cheerfully.

"I'd like that," said Addy. "Come to my house on Saturday after we make our deliveries and help me."

"Not Saturday," Sarah answered. "My momma really need me to work with her on the washing. But I can help you at school tomorrow, during lunch."

"Good!" Addy said. "I need it."

On their way to their first delivery, Addy and Sarah passed the Institute for Colored Youth. Addy stopped to pull up her knee warmers. She stared at a group of students coming out of the brick building. They were carrying stacks of books, and they were laughing and talking together.

"Miss Dunn say you can be a student at the institute when you eleven," Addy said to Sarah. "That mean you and me could be here next year and study to be teachers like Miss Dunn. Wouldn't that be good?" She straightened her back and held her head high, the way Miss Dunn did.

Sarah looked wistful. "It would be," she said. Then she nudged Addy. "But we better keep on with these deliveries. My feet getting wetter every minute."

"You right," Addy said. As they walked on, she looked back at the institute, thinking how wonderful it would be if she and Sarah were students there.

When Addy and Sarah finished their deliveries, they said good-bye and parted. Addy rushed home through the darkening streets as if she were pushed along by the wind. She was freezing! Her hat and mittens were wet, the hem of her petticoat was damp, and her feet were numbed by the cold. *Sarah's feet must be even colder than mine*, Addy thought.

She was grateful when she turned onto her street and saw the bright lights of the boarding house. She splashed through a puddle, sprinted up the steps, and landed on the doorstep out of breath.

When Addy stepped inside the door, she heard a murmur of voices coming from the dining room, though it was still too early for supper. Addy took off her hat, mittens, knee warmers, and coat and went to see what was going on.

Poppa, Sam, and Momma were gathered at a table looking at two letters. Poppa smiled broadly when he saw Addy. "Come on over here," he said to her. "I want to show you something." Poppa handed Addy one of the letters. "You know who wrote this?" he asked.

At first Addy didn't recognize the letter. It was tattered and so water-stained that some of the words had run together. Then, with a shock, Addy recognized her own handwriting. "It's one of my letters!" she said. "This is a letter Mr. Cooper sent to the freedmen's camp before you left last summer, Poppa. But how did it get *here*?"

Poppa gave Addy the other letter. "Your letter came folded inside this other one," he said. "You read so good, why don't you read it aloud so all of us can hear it at once?"

Addy's hands trembled. *Please let this letter be good news,* she prayed. She took a deep breath and began to read:

Raleigh, North Carolina
October 20, 1865

Dear Mr. Walker,

My name is Bertha Gilbert and I am a volunteer with the Quaker Aid Society. Your letter, which I am enclosing, took a long time to get here. I am writing to inform you that Solomon and Lula Morgan came to a freedmen's camp where I've been working. They —

"What about Esther?" Momma interrupted nervously. "Wasn't she with them?"

"Wait, Momma. Listen," said Addy. She continued reading.

They had a baby girl with them. I still remember them because Lula took special care of the little girl, who had a bad cold. Lula sat up with her at night even though she wasn't feeling well herself. Both she and Solomon appeared thin and frail. They left as soon as the baby was better — about a week before your letter came. I tried to encourage them to stay on here longer to gather their strength. But they said they were heading to Philadelphia . . .

"Solomon and Lula Morgan came to a freedmen's camp," Addy read.
"They had a baby girl with them."

11

Addy stopped reading. "They must be here!" she exclaimed. "They got to be in Philadelphia by now!"

"Hold on there, Addy," Sam said. "Don't be counting your chickens before they hatched. They might not be here yet."

"But they must have left over a month ago. They got to be here!" Addy declared.

"Now, they ain't *got* to be," Poppa said. "Uncle Solomon and Auntie Lula real old. They can't travel fast. They could've run into bad weather or had to stop at another camp on the way."

"What does the rest of the letter say?" Momma asked.

Addy scanned the final line. "It say she wish us the best of luck in finding our family, and she hope her letter helped us."

"It does help," said Poppa, "and your letter helped, too, Addy. Now we know Solomon and Lula on the way with Esther."

"Maybe they're here but ain't found us yet," said Addy. "Shouldn't we start looking for them here in Philadelphia?"

"We should," said Momma. "We can keep

searching the aid societies and the churches . . ."

"And the hospitals," Sam added. "That letter said they might be sick."

"I can look while I'm out on my deliveries," Addy said excitedly, "and after, too!"

"Look, now," Momma said. "I don't want you dawdling while you making deliveries for Mrs. Ford. Like she always say, she running a business. And after you finish, I don't want you running all over the city by yourself. It's getting dark early now, and them streets is dangerous."

"Me and Addy can go together," said Sam. "We can meet up when I get off work and she's through with her deliveries for Mrs. Ford."

"And me and Momma be looking, too," said Poppa. "We been working together as a family, and that's what we gonna keep on doing."

"And together we gonna find Esther and Auntie Lula and Uncle Solomon and bring them home!" Addy said confidently.

Later that night, when Addy was snuggled into bed with her doll, Ida Bean, she looked over at the *mancala*

table where Poppa and Sam were playing mancala. The lantern light surrounded them with a warm glow. Momma's head was bent over her sewing. She was fitting a cuff onto the end of a small sleeve. Addy loved to watch Momma's hands sew different-shaped pieces of cloth together so that they fit together perfectly. When Momma sewed, it was as if she were working on a puzzle that always came out right. There was never a missing piece. Addy hoped her family would soon be joined together like that, whole and safe.

"Who you making the dress for?" Addy asked.

Momma looked up and smiled. "Esther," she said. "It match the one I'm making for you to wear to church for the Emancipation Celebration." Momma smoothed the red cloth with white dots over her knees. "I picked out this here fabric a while back, but I ain't dare start nothing for Esther. It didn't seem right, you know. But now I think Esther gonna be with us soon."

"Momma," said Addy, "you think Esther and Auntie Lula and Uncle Solomon is warm and safe tonight like us?"

14

Momma sighed. "We can hope and pray they is," she said. "You say a extra special prayer for them tonight."

"I will," Addy promised, her face lit by the light of the lantern. "And tomorrow we gonna start looking for them in Philadelphia."

A MISSING PIECE

 Addy was so eager to tell Sarah about
the letter that she ran all the way to
school the next day. She knew her friend
would be as happy about the news of Esther, Auntie
Lula, and Uncle Solomon as she was. And so it was
disappointing when Sarah was absent from school.
Addy was worried, too. She hoped Sarah hadn't
gotten sick from getting her feet wet the day before.

After school, Addy put Sarah's slate and reader
and the day's homework assignment into her satchel
so she could drop them off at Sarah's house after she
finished the deliveries for Mrs. Ford. She could share
her good news with Sarah then.

That afternoon, wherever Addy went with her

16

packages, she stared at the faces of the people she passed. *Is that little girl Esther? What about that thin old man—is he Uncle Solomon?* She remembered what Momma had told her. She was working for Mrs. Ford and she couldn't dawdle. But she could not help looking, hoping to see the faces she missed so much.

Sam was waiting for her at Mrs. Ford's shop when she finished her deliveries. "I went to see Mr. Cooper at the Quaker meeting house," he said. "He told me a couple of hospitals to go to."

"That's good," said Addy. "And I got to stop by Sarah's, too."

Mrs. Ford looked at Addy with a slight smile. "Tell your noisy friend that it was entirely too quiet in the shop today," she said. "I'm counting on her to come clambering through here tomorrow."

"Oh, you can count on Sarah, Mrs. Ford," said Addy. "I'm sure she'll be here tomorrow."

"I want y'all back in time for supper, now, you hear?" Momma said. "Addy got her school lessons and her reading for the church celebration to study tonight."

As Addy and Sam headed out into the cold, Addy took hold of her brother's hand. Sam had such long legs that for every stride he took, Addy had to take two. She didn't mind. She was always happy to walk with Sam. She had missed him so much during the months when she had no idea where he was, or even if he was alive or dead.

Sam had the sleeve of his jacket pinned up. Seeing his empty sleeve always reminded Addy of the price Sam had paid for freedom. He never complained about losing an arm in the war. Addy knew Sam was proud of having been a soldier, fighting to end slavery. He had told Addy that he would do it over again.

Addy and Sam had walked two blocks when Sam said, "Girl, why you looking so serious?"

"What we doing *is* serious," said Addy.

"That's true, but looka here," said Sam. "If we do find Esther and Auntie Lula and Uncle Solomon today, you can't meet them with that stony face you wearing."

Addy smiled. Sam always had a way of making her feel better.

"Now, that's much better," Sam said. "No matter what happen today, don't lose that smile of yours."

Addy was glad Sam was with her as they

walked through the doors of City Hospital. The nurse at the front desk looked up at them. "Yes?" she asked impatiently.

"Ma'am, we looking for Lula and Solomon Morgan," Sam said firmly. "They old folks, and they got a little girl with them named Esther Walker."

The nurse quickly looked through a list of names. "Not here," she said flatly.

"Maybe they was sick and couldn't tell you their names," said Addy, "or maybe they just came in today, a few minutes ago . . ."

"Young lady," interrupted the nurse. "How do you expect me to remember a couple of old people and one baby? Hundreds of patients come through here! If their names aren't on my list, there is nothing I can do. I'm sorry."

"Ma'am, can we look back in the charity ward anyway?" Sam asked. "Me and my sister done walked nearly two miles to get here, and we just want to see for ourselves."

"You may go back," the nurse said to Sam. "But your sister must wait here. No children allowed. That's the rule."

Addy was disappointed. She sat on a bench near

the door and watched Sam disappear down the hall. In a little while, a large group of people came in and crowded around the nurse at the front desk. *The nurse can't see me!* Addy thought. She eased up off the bench, slid along the wall, and slipped down the hall to the charity ward. She was only halfway there when she saw another nurse coming toward her. Quickly, before the nurse could see her, Addy ducked behind a cart filled with linens and held her breath. When the nurse passed, Addy let out a sigh of relief and hurried on.

Addy wasn't sure she wanted to go inside once

she reached the charity ward. The room was dimly
lit and full of shadows. She could hear pitiful
moaning, loud coughing, and children crying.
Slowly Addy walked forward, searching
the faces in the iron beds. She felt sad
and scared as she studied the grizzled
old men, miserable children, and
bone-thin women.

"Psst!" Addy heard someone whisper. "Get
over here." It was Sam.

Addy didn't realize she had walked right past
him. He was sitting next to an older man whose face
was so thin, it looked like a skull with skin stretched
tightly over it. She saw right away that the old man
was not Uncle Solomon.

"Who is this?" the man asked in a weak voice.

"She my sister, Addy," Sam said. He turned to
Addy. "This is Mr. Polk," he explained. "He say he
ain't seen anyone like Lula and Solomon and Esther
here."

"But I'll keep an eye out for them," Mr. Polk said.
"If they come here, I'll tell them you looking for them."

"Thank you," said Addy.

Mr. Polk smiled. "You remind me of my

granddaughter Charlotte," he said to Addy. "You come back and see me again."

"I will," Addy promised.

Mr. Polk closed his eyes. "You better get going now," he said. "I hear the nurse coming."

"Good-bye," said Addy.

She and Sam left the hospital quickly. The cold air felt good after the stuffiness of the hospital. They walked together in silence for a while, both thinking of Mr. Polk and the other patients in the dismal ward. Addy was sorry they had not found Esther, Lula, and Solomon, but she was glad they were not in such a terrible place.

When they got to Sarah's street, Sam said, "I need to get some things at the grocery on the corner. You go on to Sarah's and I'll meet you there."

"All right," said Addy. She hurried the rest of the way to Sarah's. She knocked and knocked on the front door, but no one answered. Then Addy thought she heard voices coming from the alley, so she made her way along a narrow passage to the alley, holding her nose as she passed by the privy and stepping around piles of trash. Addy saw line after line of clothes strung across the alley. They floated like ghostly shapes in the December dusk.

"Who that coming?" a voice asked.

"It's me," said Addy. She lifted a sheet and saw Sarah standing on her toes, pinning a large shirt to a clothesline.

"Hey, Addy!" Sarah said.

"I got some good news!" Addy said. "We got a letter yesterday. Esther and Lula and Solomon may be here in Philadelphia!"

Sarah's face lit up. "That *is* good news!" she exclaimed. "Just think. Your Poppa ain't gonna have to go away again, and your whole family gonna be together soon."

"Me and Sam been looking for them today," Addy said. "I was hoping you could come with us tomorrow after you and me make our deliveries. Oh, I almost forgot. I got your slate and reader and tonight's lessons."

But when Addy handed the slate to Sarah, it slipped from Sarah's wet hands and fell to the ground, shattering into pieces.

"Oh, Sarah, I'm sorry," said Addy. She knelt

down and tried to pick up the pieces of the slate. "Now you ain't gonna be able to do your lessons tonight."

Sarah sighed. "It don't matter," she said sadly. "I won't be needing that slate anymore."

"What do you mean?" asked Addy. She stood holding the shards of Sarah's slate in her hands.

Sarah did not look at Addy. She took a deep breath and then spilled out the words. "My momma need me to help with the wash. My family really need the money. We make more money when I stay home and work. I ain't coming to school no more."

Addy shook her head, too stunned to speak for a moment. Then she said, "But you can't leave school, Sarah. You can't quit! Remember yesterday? We were talking about being teachers. If you leave school, how will you ever become a teacher?"

Sarah didn't answer. She looked like she was going to cry.

Just then, Mrs. Moore came out the door, carrying a huge basket of steaming laundry.

"Oh, Mrs. Moore," said Addy. "Sarah say she got to quit school. Please say it ain't true."

Mrs. Moore put down the basket. "Come on inside, girls," she said.

She led them into a room filled with laundry from the floor to the ceiling. Addy had never seen so much laundry in her life. It was stacked in baskets, on the table, on a chair, on the bed. In the middle of the floor was an ironing board. Mrs. Moore took an iron from the top of the stove, sprinkled a shirt with some water, and began to iron it.

"Me and Sarah's poppa don't want Sarah to leave school," said Mrs. Moore. "But times is hard, and we scrambling to make ends meet. Sarah's poppa's working, I'm working, and we need Sarah to work, too. There's just no other way."

Addy burst out, "But Sarah can have the delivery job all by herself. That way she can have all the tips—hers and mine. Couldn't she stay in school then?"

"Thank you kindly for offering to help. I appreciate it," Mrs. Moore said. "But those tips won't be enough."

Addy wouldn't give up. "She just can't quit, Mrs. Moore," Addy went on. "If Sarah stays in school, then someday . . ."

*"Addy, we got to eat today and pay for this here room tomorrow.
We can't be dreaming about someday," Mrs. Moore said gently.*

"*Someday?*" Mrs. Moore interrupted gently. "Addy, we got to eat *today* and pay for this here room *tomorrow.* Sarah needing new boots *right now.* We can't be dreaming about someday."

Addy hung her head. There was nothing left for her to say.

"Now don't go getting yourself all upset," Mrs. Moore said. "Things gonna work out. You best be getting home. Your momma gonna be worried."

"Sam's meeting me," Addy said. "I'll be all right."

Sarah walked Addy to the front door. "I'm gonna be in church on Sunday," she said, trying hard to smile. "Maybe after, I can help you practice that Emancipation Proclamation you reading on New Year's Eve."

"Sure," Addy said. She tried to smile, too. But inside it felt as if her heart were breaking, shattered like Sarah's slate into pieces that could never be put back together.

THE LAST PIECE

 Over the next few weeks, Addy and her
family kept up their search. Whenever
they could, Sam and Addy and Momma
and Poppa went to different churches, aid societies,
and hospitals. The family placed several ads in *The
Christian Recorder* newspaper. They went to the police,
too. They had not found Esther, Auntie Lula, and
Uncle Solomon, but they were determined not to
give up.

One afternoon a few days before Christmas,
Addy stopped at City Hospital after she finished her
deliveries. She was later than usual because she'd
had so many packages and errands that day. Her job
took longer now that she had to do it by herself. She

missed Sarah's help and her company, both at school and while she was making deliveries.

Addy had been to City Hospital so many times, she didn't have to sneak into the charity ward. All the nurses knew her now. When Addy stopped at the front desk, the nurse there exclaimed, "Here you are again!"

"Yes, ma'am," said Addy.

The nurse shook her head and almost smiled. "You are the most determined child I have ever seen," she said. "Where is your brother today?"

"He had to work late," said Addy, "but my momma and poppa said I knew the way here so well, I could come by myself."

Now the nurse really did smile. "You certainly *do* know your way here. You and your brother have been here so many times that you've got nearly every nurse in the hospital looking for your sister and aunt and uncle. I know it's no use to tell you that they aren't here. Go back to the ward and see for yourself. Mr. Polk will be glad to see you."

"Thank you," said Addy, and she started to run down the hall.

"Walk," the nurse reminded her. "There are still some rules that can't be bent."

"Yes, ma'am," Addy said, slowing down.

In the ward, Addy looked at each face in every bed to see if Esther, Auntie Lula, or Uncle Solomon was there. She always stopped at Mr. Polk's bed last because he liked her to visit with him. Today Mr. Polk smiled when he saw Addy.

"Hello, Addy," he said. His voice sounded stronger. "Sit down and stay a while."

Even though Addy wanted to hurry off to a nearby church to see if there was word about Esther, Lula, and Solomon, she took a seat next to Mr. Polk's bed. "You seem better today," she said to the old man.

Mr. Polk nodded. "I am," he said. "The nurses and doctors helped me get better, and you helped me, too."

"But I didn't do nothing," Addy said.

"Yes, you did," said Mr. Polk. "Your visits give me something to look forward to, something to hope for." Mr. Polk spoke slowly. "Hope is a powerful thing, Addy. It's the greatest gift you can give to somebody, or give yourself. It can see you through the worst times."

Addy thought about her own hope of having her family all together. With each passing day, her hope had grown smaller. It was now like a tiny flame. Addy had been feeling that just a puff of wind could blow it out. But as she sat talking to Mr. Polk, she could feel her hope grow bright again.

After a while, Mr. Polk patted Addy's hand. "You hurry on home now," he said. "It's getting late."

"Good-bye, Mr. Polk," she said. "I'll come see you again."

The sky was darkening as Addy left the hospital. She'd stayed with Mr. Polk longer than she'd realized. Addy made her hands into fists inside her mittens to keep her fingers warm and walked as quickly as she could. She knew she should be getting home, but tonight she felt hopeful enough to search some more for Esther, Lula, and Solomon. First she went to the church that was near the hospital. But the church was dark inside except for a cluster of candles burning near the altar, looking like stars in a night sky.

As Addy left the church, its bells started to ring the hours. They rang six times. Addy knew Mrs. Golden was putting a hot supper on the table right now, and Momma and Poppa would be worried about her. But since she was already late, Addy decided to stop at the First Baptist Church, too. It was on her way home, and if she stopped there tonight, she and Sam would not have to visit it tomorrow. She leaned into the wind and hurried along.

The sidewalk was slippery with ice, so Addy had to slow down as she approached the church. Ahead of her in the winter twilight she saw the shadowy shape of a woman. The woman was starting to climb down the church steps. She moved slowly—as if every step were a struggle. As Addy drew closer, she saw that the woman was bent over protectively, helping a small child climb down the steps. Light from inside the church spilled out onto the steps and lit first the woman's face and then the child's face, too.

Addy froze. Her heart was pounding the way it had pounded the night she and Momma escaped to freedom. On that night, she had pressed the memory of her sister into her mind—her big, dark eyes, her round face. Addy thought maybe it was hope that made her think the face she was seeing now was Esther's.

Addy saw the shadowy shape of a woman starting to climb down the church steps slowly—helping a child along.

"Esther?" Addy's voice came out in a whisper. Then she shouted and ran up the steps. "Esther?" she called out. "Auntie Lula?"

The woman stopped and turned. "Is that my Addy?" she asked. It was Auntie Lula.

"It's me, Auntie Lula," said Addy, rushing toward the old woman. "It's your Addy."

Addy threw her arms around Auntie Lula and Esther. They were both so small and thin, Addy's arms went almost all the way around them. She held on to them tightly, tears running down her face. Addy had dreamed so long, and hoped so long, and prayed so long, and searched so long that she never wanted to let go of Auntie Lula and Esther now that she held them at last.

Auntie Lula pulled back. She studied Addy's face. "My Addy," she murmured. Then she turned and bent toward Esther. "Looka here, Esther," she said. "This is your sister. Remember how me and Uncle Solomon always told you about her?"

Esther nodded. She looked at Addy with her big, bright eyes.

"What's your sister's name?" Auntie Lula asked Esther.

Esther hid her face in Auntie Lula's dress, and then looked up at Addy and said shyly, "Her name Addy!"

Addy smiled down at Esther. Her voice was trembling when she said, "Auntie Lula! We been looking for you so long! I can't believe you're here at last! Where's Uncle Solomon?"

"I'll explain about Solomon in good time, in good time," said Auntie Lula. "But now it's time to get Esther and me home."

As Addy, Auntie Lula, and Esther came up the steps of the boarding house, the front door swung open. Momma, Poppa, and Sam stood in the doorway, looking worried. But as soon as they saw Auntie Lula and Esther, the concern melted from their faces. They rushed forward and hugged Auntie Lula so tightly, she disappeared into their arms. Everyone was crying, including Esther. Momma reached down to pick her up. She kissed Esther over and over and over.

"My baby, my baby," Momma cried. "Lula, you brung me back my precious baby. You done got so big, Esther!"

Esther stopped crying, but she reached out her arms for Auntie Lula.

Addy looked at her mother's face and thought Momma was going to cry again, not out of joy but because her own baby didn't know her.

Auntie Lula took Esther into her arms. "Looka here, Esther," she said. "This here your momma and poppa and brother and sister." But Esther turned away and hid her face in Lula's chest. "She'll come around in time," Auntie Lula said softly. "She tired."

"You must be tired, too, from your journey," Poppa said. "Come and sit by the fire in the parlor."

When they were all seated before the fire, Sam asked gently, "Auntie Lula, where's Uncle Solomon?"

Auntie Lula let out a deep sigh. "Solomon made it as far as he could," she said. "He died at the last freedmen's camp we stayed in. We buried him there."

Addy's eyes filled with tears. For a long time, no one spoke.

Then Auntie Lula went on. "Solomon and me had a time of it, you hear? We had a time. The plantation turned into nothing but a dry patch of dirt. Even before the war was over, everybody knew the North was gonna win. Seem like word of it was

blowing on the wind. Slaves was running off every day from Master Stevens and 'cross the way from Master Gifford. So many was leaving, they couldn't catch them all. Soon it wasn't but a few of us left, mostly old folks that couldn't run nowhere. When we finally got news the war was over, even Master Stevens had left because he wasn't making no money. There weren't nobody to plant tobacco.

"Solomon was sick and he knew it, but he didn't want to die on that plantation where he'd been a slave. And we was determined to get this child back to y'all. So that's when we struck out for one of them freedmen's camps. Well, we got to a camp near Virginia, and Esther got sick, so sick we couldn't move no more."

"A lady wrote to us," said Addy. "She told us you'd been at her camp."

Auntie Lula coughed and took a sip of the hot tea Momma had made for her. "Lots of kind folks helped us along the way," Auntie Lula continued. "As soon as Esther was better, we pushed on. We got to a camp pretty close to Philadelphia when Solomon just couldn't go on anymore. He'd been sick for a long time, and he just wore out."

Addy buried her face in her hands, and Auntie Lula reached out and stroked her hair.

"It's all right, child," she said. "Uncle Solomon died a free man. He hoped for that all his life long. He got as close to Philadelphia as he could. He did what he set out to do. After he passed on, Esther and I came the rest of the way here. I ain't think I could make it another step when you saw us, Addy."

"You should rest now," Momma said. "And Esther should, too. I'll go up and get the bed ready."

Auntie Lula said, "Addy, reach into my bundle and get Esther her doll. She can't sleep without it."

When Addy pulled the doll out of Auntie Lula's bundle, she and Esther said, "Janie!" at the same time.

"Who did I tell you give you this doll?" Auntie Lula asked Esther.

"My sister," Esther said. She looked up at Addy, the firelight reflected in her brown eyes. "My sister, Addy."

TOGETHER

 That night, Addy was so excited, it took her a long time to fall asleep. In the middle of the night, she woke up. The room was filled with silvery moonlight. Addy sat up to make sure what had happened wasn't a dream. She smiled when she saw Auntie Lula and Esther sleeping on her bed. Addy looked over and saw Sam on his pallet and Momma and Poppa in their bed. *Finally we all together,* Addy thought. *We all here.*

The next morning, Esther and Lula were still asleep when Addy left for school. "They worn out," whispered Momma. "Be quiet so you don't wake them."

Addy bent over the bed and gave both Esther and Lula kisses so light, they didn't even stir in their sleep.

It was the last day of school before the Christmas holiday, so school was let out early. Addy was in a hurry to get home to see Esther and Auntie Lula before she went out to make her deliveries, but she had something she wanted to do first.

She ran to Sarah's house and found Sarah inside, folding sheets and stacking them in a pile.

"Sarah!" Addy exclaimed. "We found them. Auntie Lula and Esther is home with us!"

Sarah threw her arms around Addy and both girls tumbled to the floor, falling onto a pile of sheets. "Tell me the whole story!" Sarah demanded. "And don't leave out *anything*!"

So Addy told Sarah how glad she was that she'd stayed so long at the hospital with Mr. Polk. If she had gone to the church any earlier, she would have missed Esther and Auntie Lula.

Sarah sighed. "Finally the dream of having your family back together done come true."

"Yes," Addy said. "Except for Uncle Solomon, it has."

She and Sarah sat in silence for a moment, and then Addy observed, "Sarah, you got new boots!"

"They my Christmas gift," Sarah said proudly. "My momma and poppa gave them to me early. We earned enough money."

"Look here," Addy said. "I got you a Christmas present, too." From her satchel, Addy pulled a small package wrapped in brown paper.

Sarah opened the package. It was a slate just like the one that had broken.

"Oh, Addy, I ain't never gonna need a slate again," Sarah said, and tears began to well in her eyes.

Addy put her arms around her. "Don't give up hoping, Sarah," she said, holding back her own tears. "Maybe someday you can come back to school. But even if you can't, I can help you keep up with our lessons. You done taught me so many things."

Sarah dried her eyes. "Thanks," she said, holding the slate gently. "I'd like that."

When Addy left Sarah's house, she hurried through her deliveries so she could get back to her family as soon as possible. The minute she came through the door of the boarding house, she could smell supper cooking. And what a supper it was! Momma and Mrs. Golden had made everyone's favorites—smoked ham, collard greens, rice and peas, biscuits, and sweet potato pudding for dessert. Auntie Lula was too weak to come down to the dining room to eat, so before the family sat down, Addy brought her a tray of steaming food.

Addy knelt next to the bed while Auntie Lula ate. She noticed that Auntie Lula just picked at her food.

"Ain't you hungry?" Addy asked.

Auntie Lula put down her fork and shook her head. "I can't say that I am," she said. She patted the bed. "Come sit up here. I want to tell you something."

Addy moved the tray and sat on the bed. Auntie Lula took one of Addy's hands in hers. "When you and your Momma left the plantation, I was worried about y'all," she said. "But Solomon wasn't. He knew y'all was gonna make it to freedom."

"He helped us," Addy said. "But he didn't even get a chance to enjoy freedom himself."

"Let me tell you a story," Auntie Lula said.

"Uncle Solomon celebrated his freedom back when President Lincoln signed the Emancipation Proclamation. You know them masters didn't pay that proclamation no mind because the South had broke away from the North. Oh, but when Solomon heard about it, child, he came into our cabin and strutted around so proud and happy. And then he got down on his knees and thanked the Lord."

Auntie Lula started to cough. Addy handed her a glass of water from the tray.

Auntie Lula continued, "I don't want you to be sad about Uncle Solomon dying, and I don't want you to be sad when I die."

"Don't say that!" Addy said. "You not gonna die anytime soon."

"There's a time for each of us to die," said Auntie Lula. "Uncle Solomon ain't have much time in freedom, and I won't either. Addy, we don't all make it where we want to go in life. We start our journeys and have our dreams and hopes, and sometimes other people have to carry on with them when we can't." She closed her eyes and sank back on the pillows. "I think I better rest now."

"There's a time for each of us to die," said Auntie Lula.
"We don't all make it where we want to go in life."

Addy kissed Auntie Lula on the forehead, turned down the lamp, and sat by her until she fell asleep.

Two days before Christmas, Auntie Lula died. Addy's heart was filled with sorrow. She loved Auntie Lula, who had been like a grandmother to her. Ever since Addy could remember, Auntie Lula had looked after Addy and her family back on the plantation. She nursed them when they were sick. Like Uncle Solomon, she gave them advice, comfort, and friendship. Auntie Lula and Uncle Solomon had taken good care of Esther when Addy and Momma had to leave her behind. And they had used their last strength to bring Esther back to the family. Now Auntie Lula was gone. And with her death, Addy's dream of having her whole family together in freedom was gone, too.

Christmas passed quietly. Addy and Esther played with the puzzle Sam had given them as a present. Poppa had made a beautiful sled for Addy. Esther liked to sit on it and ring the bell. But the sadness the family felt over the death of Auntie Lula dulled the joy of the holidays.

On the last day of the year, their mood brightened a bit as they prepared for the Emancipation Celebration at church. Poppa and Sam left for church right after supper to help set up extra seats. Addy was supposed to go with them while Momma helped Mrs. Golden wash the dishes. But when Momma came upstairs with Esther, Addy was still there. She was sitting on her bed in the darkness. She had not even bothered to light the lamp.

"Addy, what you still doing here?" Momma asked. "You ain't even dressed yet."

"I don't want to go to the celebration at church tonight, Momma," said Addy.

"Why not?" asked Momma.

"I don't think I can stand up in front of all them folks and read those words in the Emancipation Proclamation about freedom," Addy said. Her eyes filled with tears. "Uncle Solomon's dead, Auntie Lula's dead. My dream of having our whole family together again in freedom can *never* come true now."

"Oh, Addy, Addy," said Momma with a sigh. She put her arms around Addy.

Esther came over to them. She offered her Janie doll to Addy. "Here, Addy," she said. "Don't cry."

Addy took the doll from her sister. "Oh, Momma. Look at Esther," she said. "We never got to see her first steps or hear her first words. We can't ever get back the time we missed with her."

Momma was quiet for a while. Then she said, "Remember what Uncle Solomon said, Addy.

 Freedom's got its cost. Sometimes a very big cost." Momma lifted the cowrie shell at the end of Addy's necklace and held it in her hand. "You remember when I give this to you? We were running away from slavery. We had nothing but each other and hope."

"I remember," said Addy.

"I told you this shell belonged to Poppa's grandma, who was torn away from her family in Africa and brought across the ocean to be a slave," Momma went on in a soft voice. "This shell was to remind you that we are linked to the people in our past forever. They live in our hearts. Their lives, and their strength and courage, are part of us even though they gone."

Addy took a shuddery breath. She thought about Auntie Lula and Uncle Solomon and her great-grandmother long ago.

Momma smiled at Addy. "Do you think you can go to the celebration?"

"Yes, Momma," said Addy. "I can."

When the church service started, Addy sat in the front pew with the other children who were going to read and recite. She was the last speaker. She sat still and tried to listen carefully as the other boys and girls gave their speeches. Finally, Reverend Drake said, "We all gathered here tonight to celebrate the anniversary of the Emancipation Proclamation. It contains some important words, words that are important to many who were held in the bonds of slavery. I want y'all to listen closely now while Addy Walker reads the Emancipation Proclamation."

Addy's knees were shaking as she walked up the steps at the front of the church. The words she was supposed to read were written on a scroll of paper that she held tightly in her hands. Addy opened the scroll and looked out at the congregation.

She swallowed hard. She had never spoken in front of so many people before. Then she saw her family looking up at her, their faces full of love and pride.

There was Sam, who had lost his arm in the war to end slavery. And Esther, whose babyhood had been lost to them all. She saw Poppa, and remembered the night back in their cabin on the plantation when he had first whispered the word *freedom.* She saw Momma, whose hope and strength had never failed. And though they were not there, Addy thought of Uncle Solomon and Auntie Lula, too, and remembered how much the Emancipation Proclamation had meant to Uncle Solomon.

Addy started to speak, and the words came easily. Her voice was loud and clear as she read the proclamation, with its words that had changed the lives of everyone she loved.

When Addy finished at midnight, it seemed as if the whole church exploded with joy. The bells rang out, not just from her church but from churches all over the city. Everyone stood, cheering and hugging and kissing. Addy came down the steps and moved into the crowd, standing on tiptoe, trying to find her

Addy's voice was loud and clear as she read the proclamation.

family. Suddenly, she felt a hand slip into hers. It was Esther.

Addy smiled down at her sister and asked, "Where we going, Esther?"

Esther smiled back. "Home," she said.

"That's right," said Addy. "We going home together."

LOOKING BACK

CHANGES FOR
AMERICA

A painting showing Richmond, Virginia, on fire at the end of the Civil War

In 1865, the Civil War ended after four terrible years. Families separated by slavery and by war began to be reunited, just as the North and South were joining together again as one nation. But just five days after the South surrendered, President Abraham Lincoln was shot and killed. His assassination made the nation's recovery much more difficult.

The years after the Civil War are called *Reconstruction* because of the efforts to rebuild—or reconstruct—the nation. These efforts took place mostly in the South, which suffered much more damage from the war than the North did.

After the war, Congress *amended*, or changed, the Constitution to ensure freedom and citizenship for black Americans. The Thirteenth Amendment officially ended slavery. The Fourteenth Amendment gave citizenship

An elderly black man voting for the first time

to black Americans, and the Fifteenth Amendment gave all male citizens the right to vote, regardless of race. Women were not allowed to vote in America until fifty years later, in 1920.

Congress also created the Freedmen's Bureau to help former slaves adjust to their lives as free people, since most did not have homes, jobs, or educations. The bureau set up schools in the South for former slaves. It helped set up colleges for black students, such as Howard and Fisk Universities, which are still important places of learning today. The Freedmen's

Howard University students in the 1890s

Bureau provided other services, too, such as medical help for poor blacks and whites.

Even so, the lives of most black people did not improve very much after the Civil War. Many white people in the South disagreed with Reconstruction. They were angry that they were no longer allowed to have slaves, and that men who had been slaves could now vote and be elected to public office. They were also angry that the North was trying to control the South. So Southern states passed laws called Black Codes to keep blacks in an inferior position. The laws forced many African Americans to work for low wages and made it hard for them to buy land.

Many black people who could not afford to buy farms became *sharecroppers*. A sharecropper raised crops on land owned by someone else. In exchange for using the land, the sharecropper gave part of the crop to the landowner and sold the rest to earn money. But some landowners cheated sharecroppers. This and other problems kept many sharecroppers and their families living in poverty, just as they had been in slavery.

This 13-year-old boy worked alongside his parents, who were sharecroppers.

Northern blacks, like these children in Philadelphia, faced segregation and discrimination.

Southern states also passed laws to *segregate*, or separate, black people from white people. These laws forced blacks to use separate areas in restaurants, hotels, and other public places or use entirely separate buildings.

It was hard for blacks to get good jobs or educations in the North, too. There was less violence against black people in the North than in the South, but there was still prejudice and segregation. Addy's parents were lucky to find jobs that paid decent wages.

By the mid-1870s, Reconstruction had helped rebuild the South and had given black people new legal rights. But black and white people still were not equals in American society. African Americans were often abused or treated violently, so they continued the struggle for equal rights, sometimes risking their lives. For example, Ida B. Wells, a Mississippi schoolteacher, wrote newspaper articles about violence against blacks in the late 1800s and early 1900s. She wanted

Ida B. Wells

people everywhere to know what was happening in the South. She hoped all fair-minded citizens would join her protest against such violence.

African Americans also fought for justice through their churches and through organizations like the National Association for the Advancement of Colored People (NAACP), which was created in 1909. One founder of the NAACP was the scholar W. E. B. Du Bois.

Talented black people broke through the barrier of prejudice in other ways, too. Daniel Hale Williams, a black surgeon, performed the world's first heart operation in 1893. Black musicians, artists, and writers, such as the poet Langston Hughes, became famous in the 1920s in what is known as the Harlem Renaissance. Marian Anderson was the first African American opera singer. She sang on the steps of the Lincoln Memorial in 1939 after she was forbidden to sing at Constitution Hall because she was black. In 1947, Jackie Robinson became the first black man in this century to join a major-

Marian Anderson at the Lincoln Memorial

league baseball team, paving the way for other blacks in professional sports.

Black people also went to court to fight for equality. In 1892, an African American named Homer Plessy refused to leave the part of a railroad car that was set aside for white people only. A court case followed, and the Supreme Court, the highest court in the country, decided that segregated facilities like trains, schools, and restaurants were allowed if the facilities for blacks were equal to those for whites. But schools and other public places for black people were much worse than those for whites.

Segregated drinking fountains in a Georgia courthouse

It wasn't until 1954 that the Supreme Court decided that "separate but equal" treatment for black Americans was not fair. A lawyer named Thurgood Marshall and the NAACP argued that keeping blacks in separate schools was unfair. Because Marshall and the NAACP won the case, all segregation in public places is now illegal. Marshall later became the first black person to serve on the Supreme Court.

Black students entering a school formerly attended only by whites. Soldiers kept the black students safe.

The modern civil rights movement started soon after the 1954 case because segregation continued, even though it was illegal. To protest, black people such as Rosa Parks sat in places reserved for whites and refused to move until they were arrested. People of all races protested together in marches. Many protesters went to jail, and some were killed. Dr. Martin Luther King Jr. led the effort to end segregation peacefully. He fought for justice until he was assassinated in 1968.

Dr. Martin Luther King Jr. (center), leading a march from Selma to Montgomery, Alabama, in 1965 to protest segregation

The civil rights movement brought many important changes to America. It is now illegal to segregate people in public places like schools and buses. It is illegal to prevent black men or women—or any adult citizen—from voting. The struggle of black people for equality also inspired many other people to fight for their rights, such as women and American Indians. The work of the civil rights movement continues today, as people of all races continue to fight for fairness in our society.

About 250,000 people demonstrated peacefully at the March on Washington.

READ ALL OF ADDY'S STORIES,
available at bookstores and *americangirl.com.*

MEET ADDY
Addy and her mother try to escape
from slavery because they hope to be free
and to reunite their family.

ADDY LEARNS A LESSON
Addy starts her life as a free person
in Philadelphia. She learns about reading
and writing—and freedom.

ADDY'S SURPRISE
Addy and Momma are generous
with the little money they've saved—
and thrilled by a great surprise.

HAPPY BIRTHDAY, ADDY!
Addy makes a new friend, who encourages her to
claim a birthday and helps her face prejudice.

ADDY SAVES THE DAY
The Civil War is over, but not the feud
between Addy and Harriet, until tragedy forces
them to come together at last.

CHANGES FOR ADDY
The long struggle to reunite Addy's family
finally ends, but there is heartache
along with the happiness.